Diary of a Roblox

Noob:

Jailbreak

(Special Christmas Edition)

Robloxia Kid

CONTENTS

ONE: THE PLAN

"So, it's all set, Sully?"

"You bet it is, Gravy!"

Sully and Gravy had been staying in the Roblox jail for as long as they could remember. They had been held for so long, that they almost forgot why they were in jail in the first place.

"I think it was something about robbery, wasn't it Sully?"

"It's always about robbery in Jailbreak, Gravy!"

"Oh yeah, sorry! I keep forgetting, Sully!"

Sully shook his head. It was tough having a partner in crime like Gravy. Perhaps that was why they were in the slammer in the server. Sully always considered himself the brains of their little team, and Gravy hardly ever thought otherwise.

"Well, never mind! It's not your job to think, anyway! Your only job is to get the heavy lifting done! The action and the physical stuff, that's you, Gravy! Me, I get to do the tougher part, the thinking!"

"Is that why I always get blown to bits all the time?"

Sully nodded at Gravy. Gravy was a big player. A really heavy-set kind of guy. One look at Gravy, and he seemed more fit in a gym building muscles than playing in such a tough server like Jailbreak. His physical tools made him perfect as Sully's bodyguard and muscle. He took most of the hits in their jobs, and it wasn't really that different even in prison.

"You could say that, Gravy. Well, if my plan works, you won't have to take too many hits much longer. We're breaking out of this joint, buddy!" Sully said.

"How are we going to do that?"

Sully smiled at Gravy. They were still in their cell, but Sully was pretty pleased with himself. Gravy had worked with Sully for quite some time now. He knew Sully long enough to recognize that smile. When Sully smiled like that, Gravy knew that he had whipped up some kind of smart plan. Or at least he had whipped up a plan that they were going to try and execute. Whether it would work or not, was another thing altogether.

Whatever happened, one thing was certain; Gravy had complete trust and faith in Sully. Sully was the kind of guy that Gravy knew would never let him down. They had been through thick and thin in this Roblox server, and Gravy knew that Sully was there for him, and vice versa.

"Well, I've thought of a great plan to get out of here, old buddy! After all, it's the season of giving, and it's about time the prison give us a pass! A pass out of here, and into our freedom!"

"The season of giving? What's that?"

Sully shook his head, then slapped it with his blocky hand. He couldn't believe just how slow-witted Gravy could be. Gravy was built like a truck, but there were a lot of times that he seemed to have the brains of a turnip. These were just one of those times.

"Christmas! It's Christmas time! Christmas is fast approaching you blockhead!"

Gravy nodded and his eyes lit up, with wonder.

"Christmas! I just love Christmas time! That's the time I used to get a lot of presents back home, Until I started robbing banks and people.."

"Yeah, I know you it's a great time to give and receive presents. Well, the prison's going to give us the best present yet!"

"Oh yeah? What are we going to get? Is

the warden finally going to give me the cookies I've always wanted?"

"It's going to be a lot better than that you moron! We're going to escape this prison and we'll be free!"

Gravy scratched his head. They had been in prison for so long that he had actually gotten pretty used to it. For Gravy, life in prison wasn't so bad. After all, there was a gym where he could stretch and build his muscles, and the other prisoners and guards were actually nice to him. It was a whole different story for Sully who completely detested life behind bars. Once they had been caught and jailed, there wasn't a moment that Sully didn't think of trying to escape from prison.

"So just how are we going to break out of prison, Sully? You've got a plan?"

"I just said I had a plan, didn't I? Geez Gravy, speaking with you really grinds my gears!"

"Grinds your gears? Whaddaya mean, Sully?"

Sully wanted to explode at Gravy right then and there. It wasn't his fault that he was so smart, and way ahead of Gravy, intelligence-wise. Gravy just couldn't keep up with his brain, and that was really annoying for Sully. Then again, Gravy didn't have to keep up. All he had to do was simply carry out his orders.

"Never mind! Look, I've got it all figured out. We're going to break out at the prison's annual Christmas party. The place is going to be packed with guests and everyone's going to be busy spreading Christmas cheer and all that stuff."

Gravy's eyes lit up at the mere mention of Christmas cheer.

"Christmas cheer? Shouldn't we be spreading Christmas cheer too?"

Sully knocked his forehead over with his blocky hand. If Gravy wasn't so large, he would have knocked him over with his hand, in frustration. However, Sully wasn't that dumb. Far from it. He knew that if he gave in to his frustrations and decked Gravy right then and there, Gravy would probably steamroll over him like a ten-wheeler truck. Sully would be flattened, and for what? Losing his patience? No, Sully wouldn't play it that way. For the plan to work, he knew that he needed Gravy, and just for that, he would play it cool.

"We'll be spreading Christmas cheer outside the prison when we're free. And for that to happen, you need to stick to the plan!"

Gravy nodded at Sully. He decided to just follow everything that Sully said, as always. After all, he didn't like thinking too much. Thinking gave him a headache, and that was why he left such things to Sully. Gravy always preferred doing physical stuff, anyway.

"All right, Sully. I get 'ya! So, what's the plan?"

"I thought you would never ask! Here, listen up!"

Sully began to narrate his plan to Gravy in earnest. It took him the entire night to narrate it to Gravy. This really annoyed Sully, but he bore with Gravy, and eventually managed to explain everything in detail, before they went to bed.

TWO: THE MAGIC CHRISTMAS STAR

Soon enough, Christmas time rolled around. This was the most joyous time for all the servers across Roblox, and Jailbreak was no exception. There was a different atmosphere in the air in the prison. Throughout the whole year, the guards were often busy trying to contain the prisoners. A day seldom passed without even at least one escape attempt, and the prison was true to the server's name; Jailbreak.

Today however, was very different. The prisoners were all in their cells, and were all well-behaved. Everyone was quiet, save for some who were humming Christmas carols. Normally, the cell-block would be full of guards patrolling the area. Today, there was only one guard, walking around the vast corridors. Most of the prison staff were in the events hall, attending the Christmas party. It was all, exactly how Sully had expected, and he had planned for this moment. This was the perfect opportunity to make an escape, and he knew it.

Chaz walked around the prison hallway, making sure that all the prisoners were in their cells. They were all right where they needed to be, and there was no trouble at all. He felt more than a little annoyed that he had drawn the shortest stick, giving him guard duty for Christmas. Everyone wanted to avoid guard duty at this time, and Chaz was the unlucky one who actually got it. He didn't like it, but he tried to stay happy. After all, tonight was a quiet night, compared to what usually happened around the prison.

"I guess I should be content that no one's trying to make some kind of escape. That in itself, is something to be thankful for." Chaz said, to himself.

"Guard! Help! Somebody help!"

The quiet of the night was shattered by Gravy's shouts. His voice echoed throughout the hall, and Chaz immediately heard his pleas.

"What's going on? I'd better check and see!"

Chaz raced down the hall to Sully and Gravy's cell. Sully sounded really concerned, and he ran as fast as he could.

He reached their cell, soon enough. By the time he was done, Chaz was almost out of breath. As Christmas approached, the guards were already eating a lot more than usual. That made Chaz's custom body a lot more rounder than he would have wanted. It also left him often more tired than usual.

He saw Sully lying on the floor, and Gravy bent over above him. Chaz frantically unlocked the cell door, and stepped inside.

"What's going on here?"

It was a mistake, but Chaz realized it too late. As he bent over to examine the prone Sully, Gravy swung his arm, and threw a mighty punch at Chaz. It was a direct hit on his customized body, and his body fell to pieces on the ground below. Upon seeing Chaz in pieces, Sully stood up with a smile. He was very pleased with himself, and for good reason. His plan was working.

"Too easy! I knew one of the guards would fall for that shtick!" Sully said.

"Sorry about that! I didn't mean to hit you that hard!" Gravy said.

Sully nudged Gravy hard on the back.

"Stop apologizing to him! He'll respawn in

a few minutes anyway!"

"But I didn't mean to hit him so hard, Sully! The poor guy went to pieces!"

"Get moving already! We'll be the ones who'll be in pieces, if we don't get out of here, before he respawns!" Sully said.

"All right, all right, already. Geeze, Sully. It's Christmas. You're extra grumpy, even for you."

"I'll only be happy when we're out of here!"

The two prisoners moved out of their cell, and darted towards the entrance of the hallway. With Chaz in pieces and still a few minutes from spawning, it was wide-open for the two of them to make their move. The other prisoners saw them make their daring escape, and they all cheered Gravy and Sully on.

They reached the door, and Sully swung it open. The two of them exited the cell block. They were out of their cells, but it was still a long way to freedom.

"Okay Gravy! The events hall is this way! Come on!"

Gravy heard Sully, but he couldn't believe it.

"Whoa, whoa! Run that by me again, Sully! Did you just say that we're headed for the events hall? So we're going to head straight for the party? Aren't we going to get caught with all the policemen there?"

Sully smiled and patted Gravy on the back.

"I'm surprised! That's actually a very keen observation you just made back there! You're actually thinking now, Gravy! Good for you!"

Gravy scratched his head.

"I was right, wasn't I? So there will be police everywhere, right? So why are we headed straight there?"

"Yeah Gravy, you were right! Don't worry about the cops! Remember how I was given some free passes to the kitchen for my good behavior, recently?"

"Yeah, Sully. I remember. What about them free passes you got?"

"Well, I intentionally lay low and behaved to get them! Once I got them, I used the time to spike the punch! I put a pretty powerful mix in their drinks, and none of them will be left standing! They're all drunk, or on the floor sleeping by now! That will make our escape, easy as pie!"

"Gee Sully. You really think of everything, don't you?"

Sully smiled at Gravy. He always loved a good compliment, directed his way.

"That's me, for you. The greatest, most intelligent robber here on the server! It was only a matter of time before I made my escape! Prison life just wasn't for me!"

The two of them approached the events room. Sully kicked open the door confidently. Gravy saw it, but he couldn't believe it. It was a pretty strange sight, after all.

Inside the large function room, all the policemen were lying on the ground. Gravy could hear some of them moaning, and trying to get up. None of them succeeded. Even the warden was on the floor, and he could barely make out where he was.

"Whoa! They're all knocked out like flies!" Gravy said.

"What did I tell you? I made sure their drinks were loaded! That's a fast-acting tranquilizer of my own making! None of them age going to get up, anytime soon!"

Sully approached the warden and took a bunch of keys from him. He knew that the warden had all the keys to the prison, and these would unlock the other doors or gates that blocked their freedom.

"We're as good as free men now, Gravy! Come on!"

Gravy was about to follow Sully when his

eyes came upon the giant Christmas tree at the center of the events room. It was a giant tree that was decked out with fancy decorations, and glittering balls. The shiniest object that hung from the tree however, was the giant Christmas star at its top. Gravy could not get his eyes off of the star. It was so shiny and lovely. There was something about the way the star glittered that somehow spoke to Gravy, in a way that Sully never did.

"What are you standing there for, Gravy? Come on!"

Gravy was about to move out with Sully when he looked outside the window. He saw a sight that was familiar to kids everywhere, but not-so-familiar with adults. It was a flying sleigh pulled by several reindeer. There was a jolly old man in a red suit. Somehow, Gravy heard the man speak to him.

"Ho! Ho! Ho! Merry Christmas, Gravy! Look at the Christmas star, and look into your own heart." he said.

"Santa! Santa's telling me to look into the Christmas star! It's so bright and shiny!" Gravy said.

"Did you just say Santa Claus told you to look at the star?" Sully said.

Sully looked outside the window, but the sleigh was long gone.

"The Christmas star! It's so bright, Sully."

Sully shrugged his shoulders. Gravy seemed to be acting a little strange now, but he tolerated him. Sully just wanted to escape before the guards woke up.

"It's the Roblox Christmas star, Gravy. Everyone attended the party here, just to see it. They say that it has magical powers of some kind. Something about showing you, your true self during the season, but I don't buy it."

"It's all shiny and pretty Sully!"

Gravy was rooted to his spot, and he could not get his eyes off of the Christmas Star.

This only angered and frustrated Sully even more.

"Come on! I'm not here to give you an educational tour about Christmas! We have to get out of here, now!"

Sully continued to rant and rage on, but Gravy wasn't listening to him. His eyes remained transfixed on the Christmas Star which shone on. The star was not just shining its light on Gravy. It was telling him something. It was a message for his heart, and Gravy was compelled to listen.

THREE: GATEWAY

"Snap out of it already, Gravy! Do you want to get out of here, or not?"

It was almost like a slap to the face, or cold water splashed on him. Gravy was snapped back to reality by the voice of Sully that barked at him.

"This is the last time I'm going to tell you! Come on, already!"

"Okay, okay! Sorry man!"

Gravy forced himself to stop staring at the Christmas Star, and followed Sully out of the events room. The two of them made their way to the prison yard, and finally, out to the front entrance of the jail. There was no cop in sight. All of them had attended the party to see the magic Roblox Christmas Star for themselves, and instead got a whole mouthful of tranquilizer. Gravy and Sully moved towards the front gate without a hitch.

"All right! We're almost there! There's no one that can stop us now!" Sully said.

"Really? Think again!"

They knew that voice, but they couldn't believe that he was here. Sully and Gravy turned around to see Chaz. He had his gun pointed at them.

"Chaz! What the hell?"

"Smart plan, Sully! I have to admit it was really brilliant, spiking the punch like that, and taking me out! What you didn't expect was me respawning after Gravy decked me! I'm the only jailer left standing, but I'll be more than enough to stop you two morons!"

Sully saw Chaz with his gun, and he was suddenly filled with an irrational rage. He couldn't believe that Chaz would have recovered and respawned so soon. That was one thing he didn't expect, and it frustrated and angered him. Sully suddenly acted way out of character and charged right at Chaz.

"I'll get you for this!"

"Stop! Stop, Sully, or I'll fire!"

"I'll get you for ruining my plan!"

"I mean it! Stop!"

Sully didn't stop, and Chaz fired. One shot was all it took for Chaz to take down Sully. Now, it was Sully who went to pieces in front of him. Sully's plan to escape was ruined. One shot from the jailer, and you respawned and landed back in your cell. There was no way that Chaz was going to fall foranother trick like that, and Sully would be back in prison in no time. There was only one thing that was different.

"Gravy! Gravy come back!"

In the short moments, it took for Sully to charge at Chaz, and for Chaz to fire at him, Gravy made a break for it. He managed to make it to the gate, swing it open, and make a clean getaway. There was nothing Chaz could do, but look out at the distance, as Gravy made his run for freedom.

"Got away. He got away." Chaz said.

There would be a big uproar at the prison when all this was said and done. Chaz was also sure that Sully would be furious, once he respawned back into his cell.

FOUR: IT'S NOT MY FAULT

Gravy drove down the town in his fancy red car. The steering and handling were just as he specified, and the car handled like a dream. He stopped over at the local grocery and bought some snacks. His paper bag was stuffed with groceries. Gravy couldn't help but feel happy that his life had turned out so great since the escape.

"Just another day of getting stuffed at the grocery, and what a great car I have too! I never dreamed I could ever own one of these babies, but after a lot of hard work, it all paid off handsomely!"

Gravy knew what he was talking about. It

had been quite some time since he managed to escape the prison with Sully. Or at least when he successfully escaped, and Sully was stopped unceremoniously by Chaz. The memory of their Christmas jailbreak was still fresh in Gravy's mind. The whole episode happened so quickly, and so much time had passed, but it still seemed like yesterday for Gravy. How could he forget such a scene? His best friend, his partner in crime, and his mentor had been gunned down, and he was the only one who got away? Somehow, that didn't seem fair. After all, it was Sully who had thought of such a brilliant plan.

Every time he felt guilty about what happened, Gravy tried to brush it aside. After all, it wasn't him who shot Sully. It was Chaz. What could he have done? Nothing much. The thought comforted Gravy, but only a little. He couldn't help but think about his friend often.

"I wonder how Sully's doing in prison? It

must be tough. Poor guy."

"It was a lot tougher than you could ever imagine, Gravy."

Gravy heard the voice from behind him, but he couldn't believe it. He glanced at his rearview mirror and spotted Sully sitting behind him. He also heard the click of a gun pointed at his head. It was Sully's gun, and it was pointed right at him.

"I'm touched that you sometime think about me. Really, I am."

"Sully! What are you doing in my car?" Gravy asked desperately.

"Nothing much. Just waiting for you to enter, and shoot your brains out!"

Sully really sounded angry, and Gravy began to panic. He couldn't believe this was happening to him.

"Whoa, whoa! Take it easy, Sully! You don't need to get all worked up. How did you get into my car?"

"For a guy as smart as me, it was simple to

break into your car while you weren't looking! And by the way, no need to get worked up? Really? Really?"

Sully was almost shouting in Gravy's ear now. He was really angry, and Gravy was beginning to panic a little.

"Whoa, whoa. Take it easy, man! What are you so upset about?"

"You've sure got a lot of nerve to say that, after what happened at the breakout!"

"At the breakout? What do you mean?"

Sully's hand shook as he held the gun at Gravy's face.

"Boy, you really do have a lot of nerve, don't you Gravy? You were there when Chaz gunned me down! And what did you do? Nothing! You didn't even help me! You just turned and ran, as he shot me!"

"Dude, that's not how it went down! You flew into a rage when Chaz managed to respawn so quickly, and you charged at him!"

Sully wasn't listening to Gravy. Sully wasn't really kidding when he said that he was one of the most intelligent players in Roblox. The only problem was that Sully had a weakness. Everytime he lost his temper, he could hardly ever think straight. Unfortunately for Gravy, this was just one of those times. He didn't even listen to his argument, and was full of rage over what happened.

"You didn't help me! You got away, while I rotted in jail again! You don't know how long I waited to get back at you for that!"

"Sully calm down. You're not making any sense."

Sully growled at Gravy.

"Oh I'm making a lot of sense man. I'm making the most sense I ever did in a long, long time. You don't know how long I waited to break out of jail, just to get back at you! Well guess what, you dumb ox? I did it! I managed to get out of prison, and now, I've finally found you!"

"Sully, it wasn't my fault that Chaz shot you. He shot you, not me!"

Sully wasn't listening to Gravy. He wouldn't have any of it.

"It's your fault, Gravy! It's all your fault! You got your life back, and became a success while I rotted in jail!"

"Sully calm down, please!"

"No! No! No way am I calming down! It's all your fault, and you're going to pay for it!"

"No!"

There was nothing that Gravy could do, as Sully fired his gun. That close, there was no way he could miss.

FIVE: A MEETING WITH THE CHRISTMAS STAR

Gravy opened his eyes. He had respawned, but he wasn't in jail or anywhere he knew. Everything was so bright, and there were lights everywhere.

"Whoa. Where am I? This is all so trippy."

"Don't be afraid, Gravy. You're not in a bad place, and I'm not going to hurt you."

Gravy didn't recognize the voice. It sounded distant, as if it were some kind of echo. Gravy looked around, but there was no one with him, wherever he was.

"Who are you?" Gravy asked.

"I'm the Magical Roblox Christmas Star. The one you gazed at above the Christmas tree."

"Whoa! Seriously? For real?"

Gravy couldn't believe what he was hearing. Christmas stars couldn't speak. Or could they?

"What's going on here? Really going on here?" Gravy said.

"I told you the truth. You're speaking with me, the Magical Roblox Christmas Star, and you're outside the server."

"Outside the server? You mean I can't get blown to pieces and respawn?"

The voice of the Christmas Star chuckled.

"No. This is a safe place where you can simply exist in peace. There's no anger, tension or any kind of frustration here. Just the spirit of giving that comes with Christmas."

"Sounds like a pretty cool place to me, then."

The Christmas Star chuckled again. Gravy was a very kind and simple soul at heart. It was even more than a little unfortunate that he got sucked into a life of crime with Sully.

"You could say that. You know, I brought you here for a reason."

"Really? What's that?"

"I brought you here so you could hopefully figure out th true meaning of the holidays, and maybe turn your life around, a bit."

"True meaning of the holidays? Turn my life around? I'm getting confused. This is big talk with big words. The kind of talk that Sully always gave, which gave me headaches."

The Christmas Star chuckled wholeheartedly again. In many ways, Gravy was a simple being at heart, much like a child. He really hoped he could reach out to Gravy before it was too late.

"You've been living very dangerously, Sully. You've done nothing but rob people, go to jail, break out, and rob people again. It's a vicious cycle."

"It's the only life I know."

"Yes, but what if I told you that you could live life a little more differently? See things in a different light, and live a lot better than you're living now."

"I was already living pretty good when I broke out of jail, and until Sully shot me."

"That's just it. That didn't happen at all. It was only a potential future of yours."

"What? You're telling me none of that really happened? Get real!"

This strange voice that claimed to be the Christmas star was really beginning to sound strange. Gravy just couldn't understand. How could none of that had happened?

"Of course. I'm the Magical Roblox Christmas star. I have the power of the season of giving within me. Showing you a glimpse of a possible future for you is child's play for me."

Gravy was blinded by a strong flash of light. When he opened his eyes, standing before him was the Roblox Christmas Star, only this time, the star was as big as he was. The star also had a giant smile at its center and looked every bit as giving and friendly as its name said it was.

"Hello Gravy." the star said.

"Whoa! How did you do that?"

The Christmas star smiled at Gravy.

"I told you. It's magic coming from the spirit of the season."

Gravy saw the Christmas star take shape and stand in front of him, and he was at a loss for words. He realized that he was really standing in front of a magical being who could do just about anything.

"Cool! So, everything that happened, it was like some kind of a dream, or movie that you showed me?"

The Christmas star nodded.

"Close enough, Gravy. You saw it, and experienced it, but it has yet to happen in your lifetime. It might happen if you continue on your current life."

"Wait a minute! So, if it hasn't happened yet, what about Sully and Chaz? They're still at the front of the prison gate, while I'm with you? I'm confused!"

The Christmas star smiled at Gravy. It was all a bit too much for him to take in, and it was understandably so. It wasn't everyday that you were thrown out of the server and tossed somewhere in the middle of space and time. Gravy was naturally, a little disoriented.

"And understandably so! Don't worry, Gravy. Maybe things will make a little more sense when you see this." the Christmas star said.

"See what?"

The Christmas star smiled and snapped his fingers and suddenly, Gravy and the Christmas star were gone.

SIX: THE FIRST MEETING

"Whoa! I recognize this place! I'm back home!"

The Christmas Star nodded and smiled at Gravy. They were not in the dimension outside the server anymore. This time, judging by the surroundings, they were definitely back in the server. The only thing was, they were not in the present.

"This was my home, back when."

The Christmas star nodded.

"Yes, I know what you're thinking, Gravy, and you're right. This is the time when well, let's just let it all play out, shall we?"

For Gravy, it was really lie watching a movie now. He, and the Christmas star were watching, as a critical event from Gravy's past played out in front of them.

Gravy watched in amazement as he saw a much younger version of himself, in his old neighborhood.

"That's me! That's me in the old neighborhood! I was so young! I wasn't a, a.."

"A robber. You weren't a robber in the server yet, Gravy. You were still young, and your entire life was right in front of you."

"Well yeah, being a robber and getting chased by the cops all the time wasn't necessarily my first choice of work."

"It wasn't was it?"

"No, it wasn't."

"If being a robber wasn't your first choice of work, then what was?"

"I wanted to be a lawyer, or a reporter. I

always was in the know about things. I always had an idea about current events and trends."

"You always liked to read a lot too, didn't you?"

Gravy nodded. It seemed strange how someone that seemed so simple-minded and brutish was actually a bit of an intellectual. However, that was simply how Gravy was. It was also a testament of just how much time and decisions could shape a person.

"Yeah. Yeah, I read. Read a lot of stuff. I really loved reading the newspaper back then." Gravy said, with a distant look in his eye.

"Speaking of reading the newspaper, why don't you take a look at that!"

The Christmas star pointed at the scene in front of them, and Gravy watched with fascination, as his younger self went to the newsstand.

"Look at that! There I am reading the daily newspaper! I was always so into reading the bad news of the day!"

The Christmas star chuckled.

"Yeah, that was the young Gravy, back then. Always so well-informed and up-to-date. So full of hopes and dreams. Just look at him."

The two of them watched as Gravy purchased a newspaper from the newsstand. He smiled at the salesman, and paid him a little extra, as was his habit, back then.

"Go ahead and keep the change, James."

"Thanks. Gravy! You're the best!"

"No problem! Just for you!"

"Just look at how young and eager you were, Gravy. The whole world was opening up before you, and you were so full of hope and promise."

Gravy stared transfixed at his younger self, as the Christmas star spoke to him. He couldn't believe how much time had passed since then. Gravy began to ask himself where all the time went.

"I even looked a lot smarter and sharper back then." Gravy said.

"Smarter?"

"Yeah, Christmas star! Just look at me. I wasn't as dull and slow-witted as I am now. Sully always makes it a point to show me just how much smarter he is, than me."

"Speaking of Sully, take a look there!"

Gravy watched transfixed, as the event played out in front of his eyes. It was an important part of Gravy's life, a moment he never really forgot. However, watching it unfold before his very eyes was a much more different experience for him.

"Hey kid! Read the paper recently?"

Gravy immediately recognized the young man that approached him. It was unmistakable, and he knew what was going to happen. It was Sully.

"Oh yeah, mister! There was another breakout at the jail!" his younger self said.

"Is that so? Man, those jailers must really always have their hands full trying to catch those crooks that keep escaping!"

The Christmas star noticed that present-day Gravy was more than a little distressed as he watched the scene unfold. He wasn't really surprised, but he didn't act like it.

"What's wrong? Does the scene bother you?"

"Not really." Gravy said.

"If that's the case, why do you look a little well, concerned?"

"Do I?"

The Christmas star nodded.

"You're pacing all around, and your hands are sweating a bit. Believe me, I'm the Roblox Christmas star. At the very least, I know if someone's stressed out. If they could see us, they would notice you were stressed out too."

"They can't see us, but we can see them right?"

"Yes. The past is fixed. There's no way you're going to be able to change it, no matter how much you want to. You can only look back it, with the eyes of fondness, or regret. Either way, you must look back at it, with wisdom in your heart."

The Christmas star's words bore heavily on Gravy's heart. He knew he was right, but he still took it pretty hard. After all, whether Gravy wanted to admit it or not, this was one of his biggest regrets.

"It shows that much, huh?"

The Christmas star nodded again, and smiled.

"Oh, all right! I admit it! I know what's going to happen next and.."

"..and you don't want it to happen. You

don't want it to play out, knowing what you know now."

The Christmas star interrupted Gravy, but he knew that the star was right.

"Exactly. Oh, Sully was right! I am an awful friend!"

"That's not true, Gravy."

"It is, too! If I wasn't so rotten, I wouldn't wish such things!"

"I can't really blame you for wishing such things."

"Why not, Christmas star?"

"Let's just watch how it all unfolds first, shall we?"

Gravy and the Christmas star continued to watch as the scene unfolded.

"You bet they do, kid! Those cops can be pretty persistent-like." Sully said.

"Really? Why do you say that, mister?"

Sully hesitated answering the boy's question. He didn't want to reveal everything about himself. That would be just plain crazy. However, there was something he could see in the boy almost as if, there were some unfulfilled potential within him.

"Nothing really. I just.."

"Hey! Sully! It's you!"

Sully turned. He knew that voice, and upon hearing it, he knew that he was in a pretty tricky situation now.

"Harry? It's you! Isn't that just amazing!"

"Don't go sweet talking your way out of this, you piece of trash!"

Harry approached Sully, and he threw a punch that hit Sully squarely on the face. It was a strong punch, and Sully was knocked to the ground.

"Whoa, whoa, there Harry! Take it easy!" Sully said.

Harry continued to approach Sully, like a tiger waiting to pounce on its wounded prey.

"You're not getting away from me now, Sully! Not after how you just screwed me over!"

"Harry, I don't know what you're talking about!"

"Oh, you've got a lot of nerve, trying to be coy now, eh? You deserted me back in prison! We planned that escape together, and when the jailers arrived, you just saved your own skin! You used me as some kind of a decoy to get their attention, while you just ran away!"

"Harry, no! It's not like that!"

Gravy watched the scene unfolding, and it was more than a little ironic. Harry's words to Sully were more than a little familiar to him. Those were pretty much the same words that Sully told him in the alternate future that the Christmas star had shown him.

"Think you're smart? Well, you're not, Sully! There's no way that you're going to sweet talk your way out of this now, Sully! You're going down!"

"No don't do it!"

At that moment, present Gravy and past Gravy said the exact same words to two different people. Past Gravy stood between Harry and Sully, while present Gravy struggled to somehow get his past self to hear him. It was no use. The Christmas star was right. There was no way he could convey his words to his past self. There was no way he could change his past.

The scene played out, just as it did, so many years ago.

"Get out of the way kid! This has nothing to do with you!" Harry said.

"I can't do that, mister! I'm not going to stand by, while you beat up this guy!"

Harry snickered at past Gravy.

"You've got guts, I'll give you that much kid. You're pretty tough to just talk to me like that. You don't know who you're dealing with!" Harry said.

"All I know is that I'm not going to let you beat someone up like this!"

"Harry's right, kid! You better just step away." Sully said.

"Can't do that, mister! If there's one thing I can't stand, it's a bully!"

Past Gravy's words were firm and very tough. They were the words of a young man that was full of ideals and hope. It was a far cry from what he had become now.

"I can't let this happen! I can't let this happen, knowing how everything will turn out in the future! Please, Christmas star! Isn't there anything I can do?" Gravy pleaded.

The Christmas star shook his head pensively at him.

"I know it's difficult to watch for you Gravy, but I showed you all of this for a reason. This is your past, and it shaped you to become the man you are today. This is but a reminder of that fact."

As the Christmas star spoke, the scene continued to its inevitable conclusion.

"So you're not going to move over?" Harry said.

Past Gravy shook his head.

"I'm not going anywhere. We can all settle this peacefully."

"The only "peace" you're going to get is a piece of my fist!" Harry said, angrily.

With that, he swung his fist hard towards Gravy. His fist struck the large boy, and he was knocked down beside Sully.

"I told you not to get involved in my mess, kid! Now Harry's doubly angry!" Sully said.

"You want to get your butt kicked so bad, be my guest!" Harry said.

He was about to beat them both down on the ground, but Gravy moved quickly with unusual speed and strength. He pushed

Sully out of the way, and rolled to avoid Harry's punch. Harry's fist hit nothing but air, and Sully and Gravy managed to get back on their feet.

"Whoa! How did you do that, kid?" Sully said.

"I don't know! I guess it's just a natural gift, you know?"

"You're really full of surprises, aren't you kid? Well it doesn't matter now! Defending that crook Sully was the worst mistake of your life! I'm going to really beat you up silly now!" Harry said.

Harry charged at Gravy, and threw another punch. Harry's charge was powerful, but reckless. He moved like a bull that saw red, and Gravy deftly eluded him.

"Stand still, will you?" Harry said.

"And let you flatten me with a punch? No way!" Gravy said.

"Suit yourself, kid! You're going down!"

"I'm not the one going down today!"

Harry threw another punch that Gravy easily avoided. This time however, he did not hold back. As he dodged the punch, Gravy threw another punch of his own at Harry. Gravy put all his strength and power into one fearsome punch. The punch landed hard on Harry. Gravy struck Harry squarely on the face. That was when it happened.

"No!"

Present Gravy pleaded one last time, but it did nothing to alter the events that followed. There was no way that his pleas could alter the past. The past merely unfolded as it did.

Gravy's fist struck Harry and Harry went to pieces. Sully watched with disbelief. This was the first time he had ever seen anyone knock another player into pieces with a single punch. It was more than a little unusual. He knew that shooting someone could knock them to pieces.

With all of his attempted jailbreaks, this was something that Sully knew, firsthand. You could even get the same result with a few powerful punches. However, getting knocked to pieces with a single punch was simply unheard of.

"Whoa, how did you do that kid?" Sully asked.

Gravy stood over Harry's pieces that were littered on the floor.

"I don't know. I don't know how I did that. I guess I don't know my own strength. I didn't mean to do it, honest! I was just protecting you."

Gravy sounded very remorseful, but by now, Sully had gotten over the initial shock and surprise. He didn't feel sorry for Harry, not in the least. For Sully, this was now an unexpected opportunity, and he would take it.

"Well, I appreciate it kid. Come on! We have to move, before he respawns! As you may have heard, my name's Sully."

"I'm Gravy, nice to meet you, Sully."

Sully smiled at the young boy with unusual strength. The two of them dashed out of there, as quickly as they could.

"Now that we've been properly introduced, I think we can work together." Sully said.

"Work together? What do you mean?"

"I think we can put your unusual strength and talents to good use." Sully said, with a twinkle in his eye.

"Really? Like how?"

Past Gravy spoke with a sparkle in his eye, full of and hope. He had no idea what the future held for him, and who Sully really was.

"Come with me kid, and I'll show you a really great time." Sully said.

Present Gravy shook his head with disbelief.

"That's how it happened. That's how I met Sully." he said.

"Yes. That was the first time you met Sully and the start of your entire life as a robber, wasn't it?" the

Christmas Star said.

"After we met, he showed me the plans and details of our first jobs together. We robbed the Roblox National Bank, and came off with a ton of cash. It seemed so wonderful and rewarding at first."

"At first?"

"Well, you know what happened. Eventually, at least."

"What happened?"

"Come on, Christmas star! Don't play coy with me! You've got all those cool Christmas powers. You can go back and forth in time. You know what happened."

The Christmas star smiled at Gravy.

"I guess I do. Let's go back to those times, shall we?"

Gravy shook his head.

"No! I don't want to go back to those times and see them all over again!"

The Christmas star smiled at Gravy with wisdom.

"You have to Gravy."

SEVEN: THE OLD HOUSE WITH THE BANK TELLER

The Christmas star snapped his fingers, and the two of them were transported to another time and place in Gravy's life. As usual, everything was quite familiar to him again.

"We're right at the Roblox National Bank!" Gravy said.

"Yes, Gravy. And you do know what will happen, don't you?"

"Of course, I do!"

Gravy knew what would happen, and it happened in front of him. As he and the

Christmas star watched on, Gravy's past self and Sully entered the bank. He watched as the bank's security guard tried to stop them, to no avail. Even before he could point his gun at them, Gravy threw his powerful punch at him, instantly levelling the guard to pieces.

"Everyone, on the floor, now!" Sully said.

It was a simple matter for Sully to get everyone to comply. After all, they were the ones with the guns now, and there was no one to stop them.

"Give us all your money, now!" Gravy said.

The bank teller had no choice but to oblige.

"I really shouldn't have done all that with Sully." Gravy said.

It all played out in front of them, like some action movie. Gravy watched on with regret, as his past self-committed the robbery with Sully.

"We got caught, of course. Eventually."

"This was the first of several robberies you both commited, wasn't it?" the Christmas star said.

"Yeah, it was. We robbed a few more banks after that first job. It was good, at first. We had so much money, and we could buy just about anything we wanted. That is, we could buy anything, when the cops weren't chasing us all around town."

"You were always wanted men, Gravy. Always on the run."

"I admit, it did get tiresome. Always running from the law like that." Gravy said, shaking his head.

"Do you know of the adverse effects that happened as a result of you and Sully's robbing the bank?" the Christmas Star replied.

"Adverse effects? What are you talking about?"

"When you and Sully robbed that bank, you didn't just take the bank's money. You also affected a lot of lives in the process."

Gravy scratched his head. It was all getting a little too confusing for him now.

"What do you mean?"

"Take a look."

The Christmas Star snapped his fingers and in an instant, he and Gravy were transported to another time place yet again.

Gravy looked around and he noticed that they were in a small and cramped house. The surroundings of the house looked almost ancient, as if they were from another server altogether.

"Whoa! Where are we? Looks like we've been transported to some kind of derelict of a house!"

"She lives here." the Christmar Star said.

"Who does?"

"She does."

The Christmas Star pointed towards a

young lady that walked towards them. She did not notice them because of the Christmas Star's potent holiday magic, but Gravy definitely recognized her.

"Is that who I think it is?" he said.

The Christmas Star nodded.

"If you thought that it was the teller at the bank that you guys robbed, well you were right." the Christmas Star said.

"I never thought that she lived in such an old house…" Gravy said.

"Old and not very well-kept. And by the way, she's not the only one who lives here."

"Who else lives with her?"

"Keep watching and you'll get all the answers you were looking for."

Gravy followed the Christmas Star's advice as the teller's life unfolded before him.

"There was a memo that came from you work, dear."

The voice was old and female.

"Let me see it, mom." the teller said.

The old lady handed the teller the old enveloped and she opened it. It contained a small note. As she read the note, the teller's eyes slowly widened from surprise to shock and finally, desperation.

"What does it say, honey?" her mom said.

"I don't believe this. I don't know what to say."

"What's wrong?"

"The memo says they're firing me. I'm losing my job! I don't believe this!"

The teller's mom couldn't believe what she was hearing.

"How could they do that? You've held that job for more than 3 years, and you've been nothing more than a model employee!"

"It says here they're firing me because I handed that money over to those robbers! I don't believe this!"

"That's crazy! You had no choice! They were gonna shoot you!"

"I know."

There was a stunned silence in the entire house. No one said anything; not the teller, not her mother, not Gravy and not even the Christmas Star.

Finally, Gravy broke the silence.

"How could they do that to her? Why are they firing her for something she had no control over?"

Christmas Star simply shook his head and shrugged his shoulders.

"It's just the way big business works. They're men of excess. I really don't know what else to say, but it's definitely not in the spirit of Christmas."

Gravy shook his head but the lingering feeling of guilt remained in his heart.

"I can't believe that Sully and I caused so much trouble when we robbed that bank! That poor girl was depending on that job to help her mother, and now she lost that job because of us!"

The Christmas Star placed his hand on Gravy's shoulder and said "That's not even the start of it."

"What do you mean?"

The Christmas Star did not say anything and merely snapped his fingers where they were transported to another time and place.

EIGHT: A GUARD'S LIFE

The Christmas Star and Gravy reappeared in another house. The house was even older and shabbier than the previous house. It was also a lot noisier.

"Daddy! Daddy!"

"Come here kids." a voice said. Several kids rushed towards a man inside the house. A woman stood behind the man and smiled contentedly at the children. She had a cryptic smile which seemed to hide something.

"Hey! Doesn't that guy look familiar?" Gravy said.

"Does he know? Who do you think he is?" the Christmas Star said.

"Ohh! There you go again! Stop playing games with me again Christmas Star! Why don't you just tell me already! I hate it when people play games with me! Gives me a headache!"

The Christmas Star smiled at Gravy.

"All right, I'll tell you. Since you asked so nicely." he said.

"That's the security guard that Sully shot at the bank during the robbery."

"That's him?! I didn't know he had so many kids!"

The Christmas Star shrugged his shoulders.

"Kids can bring lots of joy to a household. However, their joy will soon be shortlived as you will see."

"Why what's gonna happen now?"

The guard's wife approached and motioned with him to come with her inside a room. It was clear that she wanted to speak with him in private.

"Kids, your mom and I are just gonna talk awhile, alright? Why dont' you guys just play here for awhile."

"Okay, daddy!"

The two of them entered a room and Gravy and the Christmas Star followed. The drama played out in front of them as usual.

"This looks bad, Jeremy."

"What are you talking about, Celine?"

"I received a memo from the bank. It says that they're firing you. You're going to lose your job."

Jeremy's eyes widened, and he began to panic.

"Fire me? They can't do that! I need that job to keep us all going! What are they firing me for?"

"Apparently, they're firing you for failing to stop the robbery that happened a few days ago."

"I don't believe this! How could they do that to me? I even got shot for them, and now they're firing me!"

Jeremy was in shock and total disbelief. He couldn't believe this was happening, and so could Gravy.

"He lost his job too? Just like the teller? This is all wrong! It's just not fair! They can't do that to them!"

The Christmas Star shook his head.

"I don't like it myself, Gravy. Believe me, it pains me just to see it, but I had to show you the effects and consequences of your actions. When you and Sully robbed that bank, you didn't just steal the bank's money. You also ruined lives!"

"Nooooooo!"

It was a good thing that Jeremy and his wife couldn't see or hear Gravy and the Christmas Star. If they did, they would've really freaked out.

"I can't believe how we affected so many lives by just robbing that bank! We hurt so many people!" Gravy said.

"I know it's a bit of a lot to take in, but it's true." the Christmas Star said.

"Our actions affect the lives of a lot of people, even if we don't know it. It's kind of like a ripple effect; when you throw a stone on a pond, the ripples spread out all over the water. Or maybe a domino effect, where you topple one domino and the rest fall."

"Domino effect? Ripple effect? What do you mean? You're giving me a headache again." Gravy said.

The Christmas Star smiled and shook his head.

"Now you're the one who's putting up the act, Gravy. Don't give me that dull and slow witted routine of yours. I know you understood what I meant. You just don't want to accept the consequences and you don't want to admit that you Sully hurt a lot of people."

Gravy bowed his head and stooped his shoulders. He took a long deep breath, sighed and spoke.

"All right, Christmas Star. You win. I've really hurt a lot of people doing what I do. Me and Sully, we did a lot of bad, bad things. I guess I never really stopped to think of all the people I was hurting. I just thought of all the money we were stealing and it was fine with me. I was wrong Christmas Star. This isn't the way to live my life. What am I gonna do now?"

The Christmas Star smiled and nodded at Gravy.

"Don't worry, Gravy. It's never too late to change. After all, it is Christmas!"

Nine: Jaynine.

The Christmas Star snapped his fingers and Gravy found himself in another time and place. This time, he was very familiar with where he was.

"I'm back at the events room! The Christmas Star is gone! Or he's not... he's up there!" Gravy pointed up at the giant Christmas tree at the center of the events room. The Christmas Star stood right at the tip of the tree, where it always was. It did not speak, it did not move, and it was just there. It was just there, but Gravy remembered everything that happened to him very vividly.

"I couldn't have been imagining all of that, could I?!" Gravy said.

"What the hell are you talking about?" Sully said.

Gravy turned and saw Sully. They were right at the center of the events room and all the cops were still knocked out from the punch they drank.

"It all happened! It all really happened!" Gravy said.

"The teller! She lost her job! And so did

the guard! They lost their jobs because of us! But the future, it hasn't happened yet!"

"What the hell are you talking about?! You're not making any sense!" Sully said.

He was getting more frustrated and agitated and his friend's seemingly irrational behavior.

"Look Gravy, I don't what you're talking about but we gotta get outta here! That punch isn't gonna keep em' knocked out forever, so let's go already!"

"Alright... alright, let's go." Gravy said.

Gravy forced himself to stop staring at the Christmas Star, and followed Sully out of the events room. The two of them made their way to the prison yard, and finally, out to the front entrance of the jail. There was no cop in sight. All of them had attended the party to see the magic Roblox Christmas Star for themselves, and instead got a whole mouthful of tranquilizer. Gravy and Sully moved towards the front gate without a hitch.

"All right! We're almost there! There's no one that can stop us now!" Sully said.

"Really? Think again!"

They knew that voice, but they couldn't believe that he was here. Sully and Gravy turned around to see Chaz. He had his gun pointed at them.

"Chaz! What the hell?"

"Smart plan, Sully! I have to admit it was really brilliant, spiking the punch like that, and taking me out! What you didn't expect was me respawning after Gravy decked me! I'm the only jailer left standing, but I'll be more than enough to stop you two morons!"

"It's all happening, exactly as it played out. Just the way the Christmas Star showed me." Gravy said.

Gravy knew what would happen next, and how he could stop it from happening.

"Run, Sully! Make a break for it! I'll hold back Chaz!"

"What are you talking about, Gravy? We have to go now!"

"We both can't make it! Just go already!"

Sully knew that Gravy was right. He had no choice but to leave Gravy, if he wanted to escape and make a break for it.

"Thanks, Gravy." Sully said.

He dashed for the gate, while Gravy charged at Chaz.

"Stop! Stop, or I'll fire!" Chaz said.

Gravy ignored his pleas, and ran straight at him. He raised his fist, ready to punch Chaz's lights out.

"Go ahead!" Gravy said.

"Fine!"

Chaz fired a single shot and Gravy went all to pieces. By the time Chaz had recovered, Sully had ran away. He had successfully escaped.

EPILOGUE

"Was it worth it, Gravy?"

Chaz smiled at Gravy. Gravy had respawned back in his cell, and Sully was long gone. Everyone at the party had recovered from the spiked punch, and the whole prison was back to normal. They were only missing Sully.

"Worth it? What do you mean?" Gravy said.

"You know what I mean!" Chaz said.

"You took a shot for your friend. That's actually admirable, and I would actually respect you, if you and Sully weren't so notorious."

Gravy smiled and shrugged his shoulders.

"I don't mind taking a hit for a friend." he said.

"You should. You're going to be put away for a long time for all the banks you've robbed." Chaz said.

Gravy remained unmoved, and smiled back at Chaz.

"That's okay. Prison life isn't so bad."

"Seriously? Am I hearing things? Is this Gravy, the notorious bank robber, who's saying that prison life isn't so bad? Maybe you're the one who drank some spiked punch!"

Gravy chuckled at Chaz.

"Maybe! You won't be seeing me make any escapes soon. Believe me, I want to just serve out my entire sentence. I could even dress up as Santa Claus and spread some cheer during the next Christmas party."

"Whoa! That spiked punch must have really packed some sting! You're really speaking funny, man! You'll have to excuse me if I don't believe that last line you said."

"It's okay if you don't believe me, Chaz. I understand. After all, I do have a really bad rep. Things like that take time to fix. Respect and trust, those are things that are earned."

"I don't know what you drank, but I sure want some of it!" Chaz said.

Gravy nodded at his jailer. He could tell that Chaz didn't trust him, but that was okay. Gravy would show Chaz that he was sincere over time. He also planned Chaz by becoming a jailer himself, once his sentence was up. Chaz had no way of knowing that Gravy had developed a new perspective on things. A perspective that was shown to him by the Christmas Star.

It would take a lot of time for Gravy to fix everything that he and Sully had done. It wouldn't be easy, but Gravy was now ready to start changing.

"Merry Christmas, Chaz." Gravy said.

Chaz nodded and smiled at Gravy.

"Merry Christmas Gravy."

The End.

Made in the USA
Middletown, DE
08 November 2018